THE 'FELLA' IN THE CELLAR

Gilly Goodwin

Cover designed by Cover Creator and Mastersound Studios
Pictures supplied by 123RF and Mastersound Studios.

First Printing: Dec 2019
ISBN: 978-1-6743-2315-2

Dedication ...
To Mum ...

Who always insists that we write our thank you letters!!

THE 'FELLA'
IN THE CELLAR

Mrs Oldfield balanced upon a wobbly chair

Gold, metallic tinsel lay glittering everywhere

Small piles of Christmas cards were ready for display

But two excited children were completely in the way.

'Sam!' called his mother as she hammered on the wall

Hoping the final drawing pin was not going to fall

'Can you see if you can find – the angel for the tree?

It should be in the box in the cellar – hopefully!'

'Mummy, please can I go too and help find all the stuff?

Sam has all the fun yet he's allergic to the fluff!'

The little girl, 'Peeps,' was peeping round a chair

Looking shyly at her Mum from behind a lock of hair

'OK Sam, you're in charge, take 'Peeps' into the cellar
Be careful as you go and please try not to tell her –
Any silly stories, as you venture in the gloom.
Put on all the lights; before you leave the room!'

Sam sighed in boredom – then groaned in alarm
'Oh Mum do I have to? She keeps clinging to my arm!
She won't let me go – she thinks there's someone there
Her eyes go all wide and she really starts to stare.'

Mrs Oldfield smiled and said 'don't be silly dear –

There's no-one in our cellar, so there's no need to fear

There are only lots of boxes full of things we rarely use

A few old books – a baby bath – your Dad's old shoes

Sam turned on all the lights and grabbed the super-torch

He went slowly down the cellar steps, leading from the porch

The great explorer led the way with 'Peeps' not far behind

Travelling to the deepest cave – wondering what they'd find.

Suddenly, a shriek came from the depths of that cold vault
And footsteps running quickly, then sliding to a halt
At the bottom of the steps, the crazed son gave a yell
'Mum! Mum! You won't believe what we've got to tell!'

'Mum! There's a 'fella' in our cellar with a beard!
The 'fella' in the cellar is acting really weird ...
His belly shakes and rumbles when he tries to give a chuckle
He says he's very hungry now and tightens up his buckle.'

'Mum - that 'fella' in the cellar gave a great gigantic sigh!

He says he has been left behind and feels he soon must fly.

But 'Peeps' is sitting by his side as happy as can be.

Mum! There's a 'fella' in our cellar – come and see!'

But Mrs. Oldfield knew this joke and soon began to grin

She smiled very widely, and said, 'I just can't seem to win!

Bring up all the boxes when you have had your play,

But don't be long, the TV's on and tea is on the way.'

'But Mum! There's a 'fella' in our cellar – it is true!'

His pleas fell on deaf ears,

because tea was nearly due

His Mum was in the kitchen

preparing beans on toast

So Sam hurried back, wondering if he'd seen a ghost.

He quietly turned the corner – afraid of what he'd see

And found 'Peeps' lying on the floor – beside the 'fella's' knee

She was gazing up adoringly and laughing out aloud

Describing what she wanted for Christmas – if allowed!

'Sir – can I just ask you why, you're living in our cellar?'

He asked so politely because he looked a nice old 'fella'

'Now then, young lad – I have a sorry tale to tell

I fell when I was here last year and landed with a yell.'

'I knocked my head and when I woke, my sleigh had disappeared

I hid inside your cellar as I was feeling rather weird

I need to find my way back home for I am in a hurry

I will need some help from you, but there's no need to worry.'

'I will not hurt a single hair upon your sister's head

But I am very hungry now and would love a piece of bread

Then I must return back home or I will never be ...

Back in time for Christmas Eve – when you look out for me

'I usually get a few mince pies and glasses full of sherry

In fact I often drink so much, it makes me rather merry.

If I am quick, I pinch a stick of carrot from my deer

It helps me get my 'five a day' so I am safe to steer.'

The children went to eat their tea then filled a great big bag

They hid it from their Mum as they knew that she'd just nag!

They took it to the 'fella' in the cellar after tea

And watched his eyes shine just as bright as tinsel on the tree.

He dined on bread and ham – and he ate a scone with cherries

He drank some lovely ice-cold juice – a liquid made with berries

His tummy rumbled on and on as he ate so much food

Then he gave a great big burp – it was really rather rude!

'I need to wait upon the roof – my sleigh will soon arrive

Rudolph will not let me down; he'll get an elf to drive

I'll go back home and pack up all the presents in my sack

But there's no need to worry – I will soon be coming back.'

Christmas Eve soon dawned and he told them how to help!

They pushed him up the chimney … so hard he gave a yelp

He disappeared quickly even though he was so tubby

Then he sat upon the roof, his red suit looking grubby.

The children went to wave to him

        and 'Peeps' began to cry

She'd miss that 'fella' in the cellar

        and she gave a great big sigh

'Don't you worry 'Peeps',' said Sam,

        'the sleigh will come tonight,

And then he will continue

        his busy Christmas flight.'

As the sky grew very dark - it began to get quite cold

Rudolph came with sleigh in tow – just as the 'fella' had told

He parked the sleigh quite close to him

        and nearly squashed his toes

Then Rudolph shed a little tear and wiped his reddened nose.

The children also missed him; their friend inside their cellar
Now they knew he really was – that famous Christmas 'fella'
They almost wished they'd asked for a ride upon the sleigh
And maybe feed poor Rudolph a handful of fresh hay

Mrs. Oldfield watched as they gazed hopefully at the sky ...
Time and time and time again – she nearly asked them why?
They started making plans for a joyous Christmas Eve
Now they'd met the man himself – they really could believe.

'Let's put his mince pie on a plate and pour a glass of sherry

But perhaps just a small one –

as he will get quite merry.

We don't want him to fall again

and knock himself out cold

That 'fella' in the cellar - is getting rather old.'

Sam and 'Peeps' both lay awake – they really couldn't sleep

'Peeps' had even tried to count – herds of woolly sheep

Then the 'fella' from the cellar softly opened up the door

And left a large bag full of gifts - in the middle of the floor

A happy Christmas came and went, with lots of gifts and food

Even 'grumpy Grandad' could never spoil the mood

Crackers were pulled; the family made a very rowdy noise

Sam and 'Peeps' were thrilled to see so many kinds of toys.

Twelfth night came ... and Mrs. Oldfield packed it all away

'Gone for another year,' she said 'spring is on its way!'

'Time to write those thankyou's now – don't put it off again.

You know you have to do it even though it is a pain!'

The children gave a heavy sigh but knew that they were due
They even wrote a thank you to their funny great-aunt Sue.

Mum went down the cellar steps – to put the stuff away
She knew she couldn't put it off for even one more day.

Replacing lots of boxes ...

    ... packing away the Christmas tree...

She very soon decided that she'd need a cup of tea

She stacked them all; then checked around ...

    ... Mrs. Oldfield always fussed!

But then she found a

    Thank you ... Bye!

    ... written in the dust.

'Sam and 'Peeps'! ... Come and see ... don't tell me this was 'him'!

I may be disbelieving – but I am not *that* dim!'

'That's his thank you note' said Sam ...

...'for when he stayed right here

Perhaps the 'fella' in the cellar will come and visit us next year!'

The end

ABOUT THE AUTHOR

Gilly Goodwin is an author, music teacher and composer. She has written a number of children's stories including **Pimple's Christmas** and a middle-grade novel **Uriel … A Whisper of Wings;** the first book of a trilogy intended for readers aged approx. 9-14 … *and for any adults who have not completely given up their childhood!*

She lives with her husband in Southport (UK) and has two grown-up children. She loves all animals – particularly dogs and has recently owned two springer spaniels – Holly and Jazzy.

Uriel … A Whisper of Wings

This is a traditional adventure story (with elements of humour and fantasy) where three lively children (and their dog) are granted an inadvertent wish and embark on a strange, perilous adventure in another world. They are shocked by the arrival of Uriel, a fair youth who appears suddenly in their playroom, spouts poetry, and claims ownership of the empty treasure chest they found in the sand dunes.

Uriel sends the three siblings on a rescue mission to find the Wilton boys (their bad-tempered bullies) and to recover his birth-right; a fantastic 'treasure' – stolen and guarded by a terrifying, smoky apparition.

But who is Uriel … and why do they keep hearing the faint whisper of wings?

Uriel ... A Whisper of Wings is intended to be the first part of a trilogy and was particularly influenced by a fascination with the conversations between C.S. Lewis and J.R.R. Tolkien where they discuss the hidden messages in their novels and argue whether those messages should be deeply hidden in the text or made more obvious to the reader.

Pimple's Christmas is a charming story book to read with young children. Pimple is a young deer who can't find his family and needs some friends as he is feeling lost. He meets some other forest creatures and they all set off on a journey to find the lonely elf ... who apparently, has a clever plan!

A surprise ending finds Pimple, Rusty (a young robin), Little Lambert (a lamb) and Stella (a star) all joining together with Elvis (the elf) to form a new family. Elvis has even been given a pair of new shoes. ... No guesses as to what colour they are!

This is a story with a message (from Santa) about not growing up too quickly and not worrying about feeling different. It contains some lovely colourful pictures and images of young animals and illustrations of the key parts of the story.

A story to make you smile – with a message for everyone.

As a Composer (using the name Gilly Goldsmith) Gilly has published the first volume of a book of new and original Carols -intended for various choral ensembles from SSA through to SATB.

Count the Angels incorporates various musical styles from traditional – to light pop music. **Count the Angels** is available as a paperback and ebook on Amazon and in other bookstores. Look out for Volume two!

The soundtracks are also available on CD from Amazon.

Gilly also composes choral works/ some sacred music/ songs/ TV themes.

Please leave me a review.

Thank you

Gilly Goodwin

Pictures taken from

Uriel ... A Whisper of Wings, Pimple's Christmas and Count the Angels

Made in the USA
Monee, IL
13 December 2019